HIGHWAY WHISPERING

Hugh Rathbone

AuthorHouse™
1663 Liberty Drive, Suite 200
Bloomington, IN 47403
www.authorhouse.com
Phone: 1-800-839-8640

This book is a work of fiction. People, places, events, and situations are the product of the author's imagination. Any resemblance to actual persons, living or dead, or historical events, is purely coincidental.

© 2008 Hugh Rathbone. All rights reserved.

No part of this book may be reproduced, stored in a retrieval system, or transmitted by any means without the written permission of the author.

First published by AuthorHouse   4/17/2008

ISBN: 978-1-4343-8491-1 (sc)

Library of Congress Control Number: 2008903723

Printed in the United States of America
Bloomington, Indiana

This book is printed on acid-free paper.

ACKNOWLEDGMENTS

I wish to thank Victoria for giving me the incentive to write this book and reminding me through her actions to never lose my sense of wonder. Also, I wish to thank Heidi, Hazel, Mason, Ruby and George, my little sister Lucy, my late parents Bill and Carrie, and my late brothers for giving me the desire to persevere and find the willingness to write and not let loneliness consume me.

A big thank you to my publisher, AuthorHouse, for giving me a venue and ability to get my words, thoughts and ideas to the readers to whom I also owe a great deal of thanks—THANKS!

Now, let your imagination go free while you read *Highway Whispering*.

To all of those who have lost a loved one along the highways and interstates throughout this vast country and who have placed a cross and flowers to memorialize their passing, I dedicate this book to you and their memories.

CHAPTER ONE

Heather Shyler, a beautiful brunette with big brown eyes, and a slender physique could be a model, but that is not the direction that this young, twenty-nine-year-old femme fatale's life will take. Instead, she will soon have a life filled with the most amazing and unforgettable events that will alter her life forever, and the lives of many whom she has yet to meet.

Heather is always running late for everything, and she is always driving too fast to try and make up for her tardiness—like a bat out of hell!

Night school is just a few miles away; sure she's late for class, but she just left her boyfriend's place from a day filled with passion and romance.

I can't continue to be late like this or the professor will kick me out of his class. Steve, the professor, likes me and wants to be more than just a teacher to me, says Heather to herself.

Driving the same way each night, and being familiar with the road with its twists and turns, makes it seem easier to drive a little faster than one should, but Heather is driving way too fast.

Tom Shyler, Heather's dad, has told Heather many times to be careful, drive slower, and be safe, and he always tells her that he loves her, and that she is his life. You see, he lost his wife last year to cancer, and Heather is all that he has now.

Calling Heather on the phone is fine under most situations, but Heather hardly ever answers her cell phone, so her dad and her friends just leave her messages.

I'm already ten minutes late to class, and I still have five more miles to drive to school, says Heather to herself. Pushing down on the gas pedal, going even faster now—with no regard for what could happen—she takes a curve at 65 mph, which is clearly marked at 35 mph.

She passes a little wooden cross with artificial flowers that's kind of like a landmark to all the local people in the area as it's where a lady died years ago when a drunk driver hit her car head-on, killing her instantly.

From out of the darkness runs a deer; Heather, unable to react in time, swerves to avoid hitting the animal and loses control of her car, which goes off the right shoulder of the highway, flips several times, and comes to a stop completely upside-down with the tires still spinning.

Bill, a truck driver, is heading home to spend time with his family, who he hasn't seen since the last time he was there (about one month ago).

Bill has seen many accidents in his life, and when he rounded that curve, he saw off of the right shoulder a car upside down. Stopping as soon as he safely could, putting on his flashers, applying the brakes, Bill reached for his cell phone and dialed 911.

"What is your emergency?" asked the 911 dispatcher.

"There is a car upside down, northbound on Highway 69 about two and a half miles from Hayti," said Bill, as he ran to the wrecked vehicle. "Please send an ambulance right away. I can see one occupant inside with her seatbelt still buckled. The girl is bleeding pretty badly and appears to be either dead or unconscious."

The dispatcher said that she would dispatch an ambulance right away with a state trooper. "Thanks," said Bill, "and please hurry! I think the fuel is leaking from the gas tank and may catch the car on fire!" said Bill.

The dispatcher said, "Please don't attempt to do anything until help arrives," and then the line went dead.

The situation was much worse than Bill could describe over the phone. Almost as soon as he hung up his phone, the car caught on fire from the leaking gas. Bill was pretty much a levelheaded person, and almost always could work under extreme pressure. He realized that he had to get this young girl out of the car now—*or she could burn to death, if she isn't already dead,* Bill thinks to himself.

So Bill quickly unbuckles her seatbelt (the driver's side window was already down on a warm spring night), Heather falls into Bill's strong hands, and he pulls her out of the twisted, burning wreck just in time before the gas tank exploded. Bill said a silent prayer that this young woman would somehow be all right and survive this horrible accident. He could see that she was a beautiful woman and hoped that the emergency vehicle would hurry up.

Several days have passed since the accident, and Bill has been waiting at the hospital because he's very concerned about this girl's life, although she's still in a coma.

Heather's nurse, Heidi, is a very compassionate, caring person in her profession of caring for others. "Heather—can you hear me? I'm your nurse." Heidi carefully washed Heather's face with a washcloth. "Heather, your Dad wants you to wake up."

There is a knock on Heather's door. Heidi walks over and opens it, and there standing is Bill. "Please, can you tell me how she's doing?" says Bill. "I don't mean to be a bother to you, but you don't know how important to me this girl and her full recovery from this horrible accident is!"

"Listen, sir," says Heidi, "why don't you just go home and let us take care of her—we all appreciate what you did for Heather by rescuing her, but don't you have a family of your own?"

"Look, miss—I can't explain why I'm so concerned about this particular person's health—I wish I could put it into words—it's just a—when I unbuckled Heather's seatbelt and she fell into my arms—it felt like a jolt of electricity surged through my whole body—I saw visions of hundreds, thousands of people that I don't even know," said Bill, with a look of confusion over his aging face topped by graying hair, which helped highlight his sky-blue eyes.

"Good morning, nurse. Hello, Bill," said Tom Shyler, Heather's dad, as he walked into his little girl's room filled with all sorts of medical devices. Bill reached out and shook Tom's hand with a firm, yet gentle grip. Tom walked over, kissed Heather on her forehead, and said, "Hi, baby, Daddy's here, I love you sweetheart—please wake up!"

Heather's medical condition was not as bad as it could have been had she not been wearing her seatbelt—that simple thing that she was in the habit of doing each time she got into a vehicle (BUCKLE YOUR SEATBELT—IT'S THE LAW). A broken left arm, just above her wrist, and cuts and bruises all over her body could have been worse without her seatbelt.

Heather's hospital door flew open, and in walked Dr. Patel, a very small man with dark hair and mustache—obviously from India, with his strong accent. "Hello," said Dr. Patel, "and how is our patient this morning?" He put his fingers around her right wrist to check her pulse rate, and then took his stethoscope and placed it on her chest for sounds of a healthy beating heart. "Nurse, please help me turn her on her side." Heidi reached over and pulled Heather over just enough to allow Dr. Patel to listen to Heather's lungs. "Sounds good—thank you, nurse." Heidi eased Heather back down.

Bill felt helpless as he watched this beautiful young woman lying there fighting for her life—still in a coma. He couldn't understand what hold this young woman had over him—why he had to stay there day after day—leaving only to shower, grab a bite to eat, visit with his family and then come back to the waiting room. Three days have passed since he rescued her.

Bill is an owner-operator of his own commercial truck and has been very successful in this business over the past twenty years—driving from state to state, all over the United States, Canada.

Bill's family consisted of his little girl, Victoria, the joy of his life, who at only ten years old is extremely intelligent and loves to read all sorts of books, especially about animals. Bill calls her Tori, as do all of her friends. Father and daughter call each other several times each day, and Tori wants her dad to change jobs because she misses him.

Bill's mom, Carrie, watches Tori in Bill's home, and Carrie also lives there as well—Bill lost his dad in an auto accident in 1999, and his mom moved in with Bill, thereby providing Bill with a loving, caring person to care for his little girl. Being there gave his mom a purpose in her lonely life since she had lost her husband of fifty-seven years.

Bill's wife Tina, Tori's mom, died in an auto accident when Tori was only three years old—a drunk driver crossed the center line and hit her head-on, killing her instantly. Tina didn't suffer at all, but Bill and Tori have suffered beyond description.

CHAPTER TWO

Dr. Patel lifted Heather's eyelids to check any response to light, and there was a slight bit of dilation. Dr. Patel turned toward Tom Shyler and said, "Heather's coma is not a permanent one, and she should come out of it soon." Of course, he could not guarantee that, but was very certain that she would come out of it soon with some sort of stimulus.

Later that afternoon, Bill had come back to the hospital from a nap, a bite to eat, a shower, and change of clothes. Pushing open Heather's hospital room door, he walks slowly into the room, dark with the curtains closed, a faint bit of light shining through the opening where the curtains had not completely come together.

He spoke softly to Heather as though she could hear him, while he stood next to her bed. "I don't know if you can hear me or not, but I'm the one who pulled you from your car and called the ambulance. My name is Bill, and my late wife Tina was killed on that same highway by a drunk driver back a few years ago," said Bill. "Please come back to your family and friends, please come out of that coma, I don't know you, but when I pulled you from your car just before it exploded, you fell into my arms when I released your seatbelt—I experienced some sort of flash of some kind, I can't really explain it—I saw visions of people, hundreds, thousands of people I don't know, with the exception of one—my wife."

Bill felt tears rolling down his face as he reached out and touched Heather's hand and said, "Please wake up, please!"

Instantly, Heather's eyes opened, and she turned her head towards where Bill was standing. " Please don't cry," she said.

Startled, Bill wiped away the tears of sadness and smiled and started yelling for the nurse, the doctor, anyone, as he ran out of her room yelling, "Please help, she's come out of the coma, hurry please!"

The next few days were filled with family and friends, flowers, laughter and happiness at knowing that Heather had come back to all who knew her, but this one person, this man who talked Heather out of her darkness, *where is he, why isn't he in the room too?* thought Heather to herself.

Heather looked around the room but Bill wasn't there; she asked her dad where he was, and he said that Bill had to leave because he had to get home to his little girl, because he missed her.

"Please tell me if you have a way to contact him, because I have something important to tell him, please tell me he left a phone number or address or something?" said Heather.

"Baby, please calm down now, I have a way to get in touch with Bill. He left shortly after you came out of the coma, and felt at ease that he knew you would be all right now," said Tom.

Tom asked all the family and friends to let Heather get some rest and said that she would be home soon, that they could all come by and visit her there. "Thanks for coming over, guys, thanks so very much for all your prayers, cards and flowers." Everyone started leaving one by one, until the room was empty with only Heather and her dad embracing each other with a hug only a loving dad could give to the only child in his life, one he almost lost. "Sweetheart," Tom said, as he wiped away the tears, "I almost lost you, and the thought of that, well, I don't want to think about that. God could have taken you from me but he's allowed you to stay awhile longer. Thank you, Jesus, thank you!" said Tom.

Heather was allowed to return home after Dr. Patel was certain that she was stable enough, but had to go into his clinic for a few visits to evaluate her improvement over the next couple of months.

Heather was still weak from all that had happened to her body and her broken wrist, so her grandmother Hazel was the best person in the world to care for this special person. Hazel took care of her with such love and tenderness—Heather was so very grateful that Hazel was there to watch over her and care for her.

"Nana"—this is what Heather calls her grandmother—"I love you so very much, and thank you for all that you've done for me and Dad!"

"Oh, baby, I can't think of another place in this world that I would rather be, than to be here taking care of you and your dad. You two give me a purpose in life—a reason to want to live since your granddad died."

Hazel smiled and gave Heather a kiss on her cheek. "Now, let's get you something to eat—what would you like?"

"How about a bowl of your famous homemade vegetable soup?"

"Coming right up," said Hazel, as she left Heather's room to go and start heating up a bowl of soup.

Heather lay there in her bed, looking out of the window to a beautiful day with birds chirping, flowers in bloom, and the bright blue sky—blue sky. *I wonder how Bill's doing,* she thought to herself. *Bill's eyes are the same color as the sky—Oh, I've just got to get in touch with him. I saw visions while I was in the coma of people I don't know but this one person, this beautiful lady—she seemed to want me to do something for her, and I don't understand what, or why. I'm so confused. Bill where are you?*

Down-shifting into a lower gear, Bill is just about to go down a steep grade—Lookout Pass—a seven percent downhill run. Hauling forty-five thousand pounds of cargo can cause the truck's speed to increase at an extremely fast rate, so applying his jake brake (engine brake) helps to keep his truck and cargo from becoming part of the landscape. The day is beautiful, the sky cloudless. A roadside billboard sign on the right side of the interstate displays a bank advertisement with a young woman with beautiful brown eyes. *Heather has the most beautiful brown eyes I've ever seen. I wonder how she's doing,* thinks Bill to himself. Now he can't stop thinking about her as he descends this steep mountain grade all the way to the bottom.

Once at the bottom of Lookout Pass, Bill releases the jake brake and shifts gears. *A rest stop is just ahead, I'll stop there for a break,* thinks Bill. *Wish I could call Heather but I don't want to bother her while she's recuperating. I have some things I need to tell her about the night of her accident.* Then his cell phone rang as he pulled into the rest stop. Bill guides the truck to a stop, sets the brake and answers the phone. Caller ID shows that it's the love of his life. "Hi, baby, how are you today?"

"I'm fine, Daddy, I miss you—when are you coming home? Please come home soon, Daddy!" says this little person who loves her daddy so very, very much.

"I'll be on my way back sometime in the morning, baby, after I deliver this load, then I'll pick up another load and start my way back home," says Bill. "How's your grandmother doing?"

"She's fine, she wants me to tell you to be careful, and she sends her love, too!" says Tori.

"Tell her that I love her and that I am always careful, 'cause I have you two to come home to! I love you, baby, and don't worry!" said Bill.

"Have you heard from Heather's family since I left?" asked Bill. "I left our phone number with Heather's dad just before I left the hospital."

"No, sir—she hasn't called," said Tori. "Daddy, please find another job if you can, I miss you so much—I have friends whose fathers are home every night, and I want you home with me, too!"

Bill's heart warms with the thought that this little person wants him with her like all the other dads. "Honey, if I could find something else, I would," said Bill. We'll talk about it when I come home this time, all right?" said Bill.

"Promise?"

"I promise, sweetheart."

"All right, Daddy, I'll let you go, and please be careful. I love you."

"I love you too, honey," said Bill.

Bill has been wanting to find something else to do for a living since his wife died years ago, but hasn't found that particular job yet that would cover the cost of raising a little girl.

Heather—what are you doing now? Bill wondered to himself—while Heather's thoughts turned to Bill.

Why am I thinking so much about this stranger who just happened to come into my life when I needed help so desperately? she thought to herself. *Who was the beautiful blond lady in my dreams who seemed to beckon me to help her? Who are all those other people—hundreds—all whispering something softly, something I can't quite remember...* "Why—who is she?" Heather mumbles aloud just as Nana walks into the room with her famous soup.

"Who were you talking to?" Hazel asked her granddaughter with a smile.

"Oh, I was just thinking about that man—Bill, the man who saved my life." Heather sighed.

"Here, honey, eat your soup so you can get your strength back. I want you back healthy and strong like before the accident, all right?" said Hazel.

"All right, Nana," says Heather.

"It was a miracle that Bill stopped that night to help you from that wreck. I couldn't bear the thought of not having you in my life, and your dad would be devastated too, since your mom died. I'm so grateful that I have you and your dad to take care of," said Hazel.

* * * * * * * *

"Dad might get another job when he returns this time," said Tori. "I called him awhile ago, and he said that we would talk about it when he comes home from this trip. Oh, I miss Daddy so, so much—and all of my friends have their dads home each night, and they have their moms, too. Grandmother, tell me about my mom. I remember her holding me in the same hospital that that lady was in that Dad helped a few days ago. What was her name?"

"Heather," says her grandmother.

"Oh, yeah," says Tori. "Heather. Mom had gotten sick and had to go to that hospital. I remember her holding me, and telling me that she loved me more than life itself. I miss my mommy, and she sometimes visits me in my dreams. She tells me that she loves me, and that she's proud of me, and for me not to worry, that we'll be together again someday." Carrie feels the tears starting to fall from her eyes, and reaches out and embraces her little grandchild, and they comfort each other.

"Can I go and meet Heather someday, Grandmother?" asks Tori.

"I think we should ask your dad when he returns home. Would that be all right?"

"Sure," says Tori with a big smile.

CHAPTER THREE

Adam, Heather's boyfriend, was a very irresponsible individual with no set plan for his life. Only working a meager job, earning just enough to pay his bills, Adam lacked ambition to better himself, which irked Heather immensely. He was good-looking, had a good body, and he exercised all the muscles in his body, but not the one between his ears.

Heather had notions of breaking off their relationship, but held off because he was a *hottie* and desired by many other women. Since her accident, Heather had some time to rethink her life, and Adam didn't seem to be in the picture, so Heather decided to tell him, when she got back on her feet, that it was time to go their separate ways.

Bill will be home soon and gets more excited with each turn of the wheels. He's always thrilled when he's on his way home to his little girl and his mother—his little family.

I think I'll call Tom Shyler and ask him if Heather is getting better, Bill thought. He dialed the number that Tom gave him that last day at the hospital. The phone rang—once, twice, three times, and then four—Bill had almost hung up when he heard a voice say, "Hello." *It's Heather.*

After a long pause, the hair stood up on Bill's arms when he heard this person on the other end. "Hello, this is Bill Wilson, is ah—ah Heather there?"

Heather's heart almost skips a beat and she feels flush and almost shy at hearing Bill's voice. " Ah—hello, Bill. How ah—are you?" Heather is finally hearing this knight on a white horse who saved her life, only for the second time since her accident, now on the other end of a phone. "This is Heather speaking—how are you, Bill? I have so many things to say to you, and I want to start by saying—thank you for saving my life!

"Where are you now, Bill?" says Heather almost in a frantic hurry to speak to this man who has occupied almost every waking thought since she came out of her coma.

"Well," says Bill with a lump welling up in his throat, "I'm about one hundred miles out of Hayti and should be home in about two hours or so. How are you doing, Heather? I mean, talk about lousy timing—I had to go back to work right after you came out of your coma, and I had so much to say to you, and ah well, Heather, I'm sorry, please forgive my manners. I'm doing all the talking, and ah, I get so lonely out here on the road for such a long time, just to hear another voice on the other end of my phone is, ah well, it's really nice!" said Bill with an excitement that he hasn't felt in many years.

Heather thinks to herself, *This man holds the answer to many questions, and he's obviously as nervous as I am.* "Bill, do you remember the day that I woke up from the coma, and you were, ah, ah"—she expelled the oxygen from her lungs in a sort of nervous pause—"crying?"

"Yes," said Bill with a sort of reluctance to talk about it. "I remember I was so happy and excited that you were going to be all right that I ran out of the room yelling for someone to kinda come and validate that I wasn't dreaming myself," says Bill with a smile so big he couldn't remember the last time he had smiled like that.

Hearing Heather talking to someone on the phone, Hazel walks back into her granddaughter's room to investigate a little. Hazel whispers, "Who are you talking to?"

"Bill!" says Heather with a big smile almost covering her face. Heather is actually glowing at the reality of really talking to this intriguing man on the phone.

Bill hears her talking to someone else and says, "Oh, I'm sorry I didn't know you were busy." *I mustn't forget my manners,* thinks Bill to himself. "I can call you back later when I get into town and get settled in if you like?"

"No, No, please continue—now that I'm truly able to talk to you, I don't want you to hang up unless you really need to go," said Heather.

"Sure of course," said Bill, Thinking, *This mysterious person actually wants to talk to me as though she's interested in what I have to say.* "I can talk as long as you like, Heather." And they talked for the next two hours about many things, including the night of the accident.

"Heather, I've driven all over the U.S. and Canada, and I've seen hundreds of accidents, and yours was right up there as being one of the worst. God was watching out for you," said Bill with a convincing tone in his voice that said he knew exactly what he was talking about.

"My late wife died on that same stretch of highway—Highway 69. She was hit head-on by a drunk driver almost seven years ago. My daughter, ah our daughter, was only three at the time," said Bill with a willingness to talk to an almost total stranger about something so painful. "Please forgive me. I'm not used to talking about my late wife to people I hardly know but you are most certainly an exception."

Heather almost interrupts him and asks, "What was her name?"

"Tina," said Bill.

"When I was still in a coma I saw so many people all whispering things to me all at the same time I couldn't understand what they were saying, but this one person, this beautiful lady, approached me and was wearing a blue jogging suit and she had blond hair and blue eyes."

Bill's heart almost stopped beating; he was shocked at what Heather was telling him.

"I must meet with you in person as soon as possible, Heather! Please, if you don't mind, because what you just told me was a description of what my late wife was wearing the day she died she. Tina had blond hair and blue eyes," said Bill almost frantically.

"Of course. Bill, can you come over tomorrow morning to my place? I'll introduce you to my grandmother, Hazel, she's here taking care of me since my accident. My dad travels a lot, and he may be home when you come over. I'll introduce you to him too."

"I've already met your Dad, uh I mean Tom," said Bill.

Both Heather and Bill were so thrilled at the knowledge that they would actually be talking in person within the next fifteen to twenty hours, with so much to say and answers to so many questions, that they could hardly contain the excitement within themselves.

Time seemed to almost stand still for the meeting between these two people who are as uncertain about what's happening in their lives as two people could be since the instant their bodies touched each other when Heather fell into Bill's arms the night he pulled her from a certain death.

Why these two people? Why now, and why are they forever more connected to each other in a story that will continue to unravel mystery after mystery with each passing day? Read on, and you will find out with each turn of the page.

The sun has started coming over the trees, and soon it will be time to drive over to meet Heather. *I'm so nervous, I haven't felt like this in years*, thought Bill to himself. He had a warm welcome home last night and a good home-cooked meal that his mom made for the three of them. Tori was so happy that he was back for a few days and that he was going to meet and talk with this lady named Heather. "Can I go with you, Daddy, I'd like to meet her too!" *said Tori with a similar bit of excitement that her dad seemed to be expressing.*

"Baby, let me go first and kinda break the ice so to speak, and the next time you can go, okay?" said Bill to his little girl, the absolute love of his life.

"OH okay," said Tori with a reluctant yet understanding tone in her little voice.

Bill had hardly slept at all at just knowing that he would soon be in front of this beautiful woman who has haunted his dreams since he first came into contact with her. All night long he found himself looking over at his alarm clock to make certain that he didn't over sleep even though he had set the alarm to wake him at 6AM. Not trusting himself that he had truly set the alarm, Bill kept checking to make absolutely certain that the alarm was really set.

First was a click, and then the alarm was sounding with a loud buzzing that woke Bill from a deep sleep, and he jumped straight up and out of bed.

It seems like I just lay down a few minutes ago… WOW, what a restless night, thought Bill to himself. When he's home he always goes into Tori's room and stands beside her bed to kind of check on his precious little person. He looks at her from the top of her head sticking out from under the covers to her little feet hidden within the folds of her most favorite blanket, the blanket that was her mother's when she was a little girl, a blanket with Teddy Bears all over it.

Tina, if you can hear me, our little girl is growing up, and she looks so much like you. You would be so proud of her. All of God's children are precious, and I was blessed to have had you in my life for a while, Tina, and when you left, you left a little part of yourself here with me—a little you—Tori. I still love you, Tina, and I miss you, baby, thinks Bill at Tori's bedside, and then he leans down and gently kisses his little girl on the top of her head.

Bill showers and shaves, gets dressed, then walks into the kitchen where his mom is busy cooking up a breakfast for her little boy and her granddaughter. "Good morning, son, how 'bout a cup of coffee and breakfast?" says Carrie to her only child. "Just a cup of coffee, Mom, I'm too nervous to eat anything," says Bill, as he pours a cup of coffee and doctors it with artificial sweetener.

Bill walks over to his dutiful mother and gives her a hug and kiss. "I love you, Mom. Thanks for everything you do for Tori and me. We'd be totally lost without you here with us!" said Bill.

"Oh dear. Don't think a thing about that. I should be thanking you for letting me stay here with you and Tori. After your dad died I was so scared at the thought of being all along and then you and Tori asked me to come and stay here. Honey, it gave me a willingness to continue on," said Carrie while pouring herself another cup of coffee.

Tori walks into the kitchen rubbing her eyes, stretching, and yawning and reaches out to her dad, giving him a hug, then over to her grandmother for the same. "Can I have oatmeal this morning with cinnamon and toast?" says this little person with another big stretch and yawn.

"Already working on that, baby, give me about three more minutes and it'll be ready," says her grandmother as she opens the refrigerator to get the butter for the oatmeal.

"Are you excited about meeting the lady you rescued, Daddy?" asks Tori as she picks up a glass of milk to drink. "Tell her I said hello, please, and that I can't wait to meet her too." This little person takes a drink, leaving a line of milk over her upper lip.

"I will, baby, I promise," said Bill about his meeting this morning with Heather. He can hardly contain himself.

His mom notices, saying, "Honey, please sit down and eat something, maybe read the paper or something. Have another cup of coffee."

"All right, Mom, I'll have another cup of coffee." He reaches for the pot to pour into his empty cup.

"Bill, you're making me nervous too. Calm down," says his mom.

Her only child sits down, smiling at his mom and little girl. He takes a deep breath, exhales, takes a sip of coffee, and tries to get his nervousness under control.

Meanwhile, on the other side of town Heather is busy getting ready for this all-important meeting. Hazel has been up for a couple of hours as she is an early riser and early to bed sort of person.

"Nana," calls out Heather to her busy grandmother. "What should I wear, jeans or a dress or ah… oooohhhh. I'm so nervous!"

"Honey, just wear jeans and shirt. Dress comfortable. I'm certain Bill won't mind what you're wearing, so calm down, dear."

Hazel is from Great Britain and has had to completely change her lifestyle. Being from an extremely wealthy and well-connected family who has a history going back hundreds of years, Hazel has lived a privileged life and has had many meetings with members of the royal family.

Hazel's late husband, Alexander, died from prostrate cancer while in the Queen Elizabeth Hospital in King's Lynn near the royal estate of Sandringham.

Although Hazel is aware that there's a possibility that she could get lung cancer, she continues to smoke with her cigarette protruding out the end of a long cigarette holder, though only smoking outside, respecting the home that she shares with her granddaughter and son.

Hazel has the resources to buy whatever she wants, and of course Heather knows her grandmother is well-to-do. Heather never mentions that fact to anyone.

Hazel and her late husband, Alexander, had one child, a boy named Tom, who went against his parents' wishes and married an American girl named Ruby. Ruby had gone to university in England and was out one night on a weekend and met Tom, and it was love at first site.

Tom and Ruby did finish college, and they lived in England part of the year and in the town of Hayti, Missouri, where Ruby's family lives, for part of the year.

Of course, there were questions about this Englishman whom she had married and brought home with her, but they kept a low profile and didn't flaunt their privileged way of life. Also, this marriage was kept out of the English tabloids in order to keep imaginations in check, which was not an easy thing to do because Ruby was well liked among the young men in both countries.

After their lives were sort of settled to where people for the most part stopped asking questions, Heather was born of that union on May 11, 1976. She was a truly happy baby girl who grew into a bit of a tomboy in some respects.

Tom's parents were wealthy land owners in England and had many of the local villagers working for them; in return they received free rent and a pay packet each week. English owners of large tracts of land are most often farmers who employ local villagers for things ranging from doing the farming to cleaning their big, expansive homes, etc.

Tom's father, Alexander, owned a large produce company in the village of Syderstone, in the County of Norwich, and had to travel to promote his business and ship its products to grocery stores all around Europe, Australia, and parts of eastern United States.

When Alexander died, it all but devastated his wife, Hazel. He was her life and her shining knight who gave her a lifestyle that was the envy of all who knew her with the exception of a few. After the funeral, Hazel would not let her little boy, Tom, out of her sight for very long as he was all that remained of a physical connection to her late husband.

Tom grew up knowing his father's business from the inside out, and after he graduated from Cambridge University with a degree in Business Management, he took the helm of the vast business that has provided a more than generous life for he and his wife Ruby and employed hundreds of local villagers and many in other countries.

CHAPTER FOUR

Many happy days filled Tom and Ruby's lives, and the happiest was when their daughter Heather was born. The saddest day was when Ruby died of cervical cancer with her loved ones around her bedside.

Ruby and Tom had many discussions before she died, and most were regarding Tom and their daughter Heather. "Please carry on with your lives and do not be depressed at my passing," she said on one occasion, and that truly was hard for Tom to agree to do as she was his life and vice-versa, but he did agree, knowing full well that he could never find another after having the best wife a man could possibly ever be blessed with.

Another request was that Heather be brought up in her little town of Hayti, Missouri, to let her grow up in an environment of an American lifestyle, part of the time and travel to the old country (England), to live at the old English home place, the remainder of the year. Tom completely agreed to do this without reservation, as he loved that little town where his true love was born and lived until she traveled to England to attend university when she and Tom met each other and fell in love and married.

Tom was about to leave on a long trip abroad when his little girl had her accident. He canceled all plans and meetings until further notice, turning all business matters over to his senior vice-president. This brush with death of his only child, Heather, was a jolt to his priorities, and he made known to all that his little girl was more important than all other things in his life.

Hazel lived in England most of the time and just happened to be visiting in Hayti, when this horrible accident took place.

Tom asked his mother to please stay a bit longer and help take care of this most important young lady. Of course, Hazel couldn't refuse as Heather was her only grandchild and meant more to Hazel than all of the wealth that her late husband left her when he died.

Bill is driving to a part of town that he seldom has gone to with the exception of looking at the huge estate that was well known to all in the area. A life of privilege is what he thought to himself as he topped the hill and saw in the valley below the large, English-style rock mansion with a tree-lined entrance to a circular driveway with a fountain in the center.

How the other half lives, thought Bill to himself, as he parked his pickup.

Out from the massive doors that were apparently the front door came the servants who were more than ready to finally meet the man who saved this young lady that all adored.

First to greet Bill was Tom Shyler; they shook hands, and as a sign of warm affection for saving his little girl, Tom gave Bill a hug of appreciation with a "Thank you again" from the man who had developed a high respect for Bill.

After entering through the massive foyer, Tom led Bill into the drawing room where his mother and daughter were waiting with a few other friends.

Bill's eyes scanned the group of strangers, and his visual quest stopped when he saw Heather. He smiled as he was introduced to Hazel, and she embraced Bill with a hug much like Bill has received in the past from his own mother. "Oh Bill, I can't begin to tell you how much this family appreciates what you did to save our little girl that horrible night!" said Hazel with a smile that Bill could see was from her heart.

The group of friends and Tom all started applauding and cheering.

Bill blushed as he could feel the blood swell up in his face, not really embarrassed, but he had never been in a situation like this before. He wasn't the sort of person to blush, but this time he did, and it was obvious to all in attendance.

Tom broke the applause with, "That's enough, everyone. I think Bill might like to have something to drink—I know I would, so, everyone, let me make a toast." As the manservant served a glass of champagne to all present, Tom raised his crystal glass into the air and said, "To Bill, the hero who saved the most precious person in my (our) lives!"

"*Hear! Hear!*" shouted the group of friends and family. Bill blushed again as he took a sip of the liquid nectar.

Bill looked to see if Heather was looking at him, hoping that she hadn't seen him blush, because he was not the kind of man to be embarrassed by much of anything. He has had a hard life and has seen much heartache, so it kind of left him a bit hard around the edges.

Heather walked over to Bill and looked into his eyes. She smiled and said, "Thank you for saving my life, Bill," as she gave him a warm embrace.

Bill responded in kind with, "I'm glad you're all right, Heather. I've seen many accidents and helped in a lot of those, but never have I experienced a situation like the one with you." You could tell that these two individuals had much to say to each other and couldn't wait until these festivities were over.

After a couple of hours the group started leaving one by one, and then there were only four in the massive room: Tom, Hazel, Heather and Bill.

Tom said to the remainder in the room, "Let's have a seat—Mother and I have something we want to tell you, Bill, and you might want to be sitting down when we tell you." Bill had a confused look about his face, not knowing what to expect as he sat down next to Heather on a plush sofa.

"Mother, won't you say a few words now?" Tom gave way to the person who gave him life and for whom he had much respect.

"Bill, I think you've gathered how much Heather means to this family and the act of you stopping that horrific night to save this precious, precious person of ours can't and will not go unrewarded.

"Tom and I have done a little investigating and have found that you've been a self-employed truck driver and you—well—uh—your."

Tom, interrupting, says, "What Mother is trying to say is we're very interested in helping to expand your business."

Bill's not completely certain about what he's hearing, as he's a self-made man. "I don't understand what you're saying—I, uh—you, uh, want to help me expand my business?" said Bill with a bit of uneasiness. "Look, I only stopped to help her, and I did, and now Heather's all right, and that's wonderful, but I didn't do it for anything in return. I stopped that night because that's the type of person I am. I don't ask for help in my business—I'm doing quite well, you see. Of course, not as well as all of you, but I take care of my little girl and my Mom and we are all right," said Bill with a sort of defiant tone in his voice.

Hazel interrupted, saying, "My late husband—Tom's father—ran a very successful business, and now Tom is at the helm. He's been running this business since Alexander died many years ago—you see, Bill, our company is in the trucking business as well, except on a much larger scale," said Hazel in a tone of voice as to not sound like she was boasting but just telling about their empire. "This family has resources that are extremely vast as we are a multi-national, or should I say a global business, in that we own and operate produce factories and thousands of acres of farmland in Europe growing produce, with our headquarters in England in the village of Syderstone. This business keeps Tom traveling most of the time, but when we almost lost Heather—well, Bill, when we came close to losing our little girl, and you saved her from certain death—we can not and will not let this deed go unrewarded!" said a very convincing matriarch.

"I don't know what to say—I uh—I'm not concerned about being rewarded. I stopped to help an accident victim, that's my nature to help. Heather and I have experienced something and that we've got to find what it is, is what's brought us to this point," said Bill.

Heather agreed with Bill. "Bill and I need to discuss some things. Dad and Nana, please can we have some time alone for a while to talk please?"

"All right then, but this matter of a compensation is not over, dear—we will talk more about it later, and that's final!" exclaimed Hazel with a tone that was resolute and certain.

"Okay—okay," said Heather, as Heather led Bill by hand into another room to be alone, just the two of them to discuss many things, especially the visions of people they both saw and can't explain, and one person in particular—Bills late wife, Tina.

Tom and his mother talked a while longer about how to get Bill to agree to this reward they're offering. "Tom, I respect this man. I know he just stopped to help a defenseless person, but this person just happens to be my granddaughter and your daughter. We've both lost loved ones—Alexander and Ruby—and we almost lost our dear Heather, but thanks to this wonderful man, this seemingly selfless individual who risked his own life to save our little girl—Tom, we've got to reward this bravery!"

"I agree, Mother, and we will find a way to get him to accept!" said Tom as he took another sip from the crystal wine glass.

Heather and Bill started to get comfortable with being alone for truly the first time since just before Heather came out of her coma.

Tom and Hazel were feeling confident in the fact that they would succeed in their attempt to get Bill to agree to compensation.

Meanwhile, back in another part of Hayti, on the other side of town and across the tracks, out in the country on a twenty-acre plot of land that Bill and Tori and Carrie calls home, Tori and Carrie are sitting out on the front porch talking about Bill and wondering what he's doing over on the other side of the mountain at that most beautiful palace with the horses and stables and many other animals including dogs—Tori's favorite animal.

"Grandmother, I wish I could have a dog like the people have where Daddy is now. A Siberian Husky with blue eyes, that's my favorite type of dog," Tori told her grandmother, who was holding this little person by her tiny hands. Tori remembers driving with her dad out into the country to see this beautifully landscaped part of town with the horses and the dogs. Not just any dog but Siberian Huskies, her favorite dog breed. "I want a girl dog and to name her Terra," said Tori as she looked at her grandmother.

"Baby, I'm certain that someday your dad will let you have that dog you want so badly, but don't get your hopes up too high because owning a pet is a real responsibility, and he wants to make certain that you'll be a good pet owner," said Carrie to her little granddaughter who now seemed a little sad at the thought of maybe not getting the dog of her dreams.

"I can take care of a dog, I promise I can!" exclaimed Tori at the thought of not having a little pet of her dreams. "Oh—I just have to have a Siberian Husky. They're so beautiful, and would make a great pet!" reaffirmed Victoria to her very sympathetic grandmother.

A comfortable breeze came through the trees, across the yard, and over the porch where these two sat still holding hands. The scent of roses and other flowers was in the air as if to remind these two of Tori's late mother—Tina. "Your mother loved roses," said Carrie as she breathed in deeply to capture the sweet smell of one of Mother Nature's favorite scents.

Tori leaned her little head back and with her nose in the air she took a deep breath with her mouth closed, savoring that special, distinctive scent that was her mother's favorite. "Mmm—I like that. Can we go and cut some roses and give them to Daddy when he comes home from that meeting?" said Tori with a smile of innocent love beaming from her beautiful face.

"Of course we can, sweetheart. I think that would be a wonderful idea. I know your dad will love the roses, especially knowing that they came from you!" said Carrie with a big grin as she stood up with Tori's hand in her hand, and they both walked over to where the roses were on the far corner of the yard.

"Bill, would you care for something else to drink?" said Heather as she walked over to the window and looked out across the expansive estate.

"No thanks, I'm fine," said Bill as he walked over to where she was standing.

"You know, Bill, I think the night of my accident—only for an instant—I saw a cross with flowers that's been there for several years, and uh…well, it's kind of a landmark, or at least that's how I see it. I mean I know someone died at that spot in some kind of accident, but I have over the years just sort of come to look at it as a landmark. Do you know what I'm trying to say?" said Heather with a confused look on her face.

"The only cross with flowers on it that's in the same area where your accident took place is…" Bill took a long pause before he said, "…where my late wife died seven years ago. I put the cross there and change the flowers every other month or so. Heather, you said earlier that you saw a blond lady with a blue jogging suit while you were in the coma, is that right?"

"Yes that's right," reaffirmed Heather as she shook her head up and down in agreement. "Bill, I'm so very, very sorry, I had no idea that it was your wife that died there!" said an apologetic Heather.

"There's no way you could've known, Heather. Don't worry about it," said Bill, realizing that Heather was concerned and seemed upset.

Heather continued, "She was moving her mouth as though she was trying to tell me something, and uh—she reached out to touch my hand.

"I don't know who all the other people were, but—can I call her Tina?—she was right there, just as close to me as you and I are now, and all the others were everywhere," said Heather as she gazed with a stare of disbelief into Bills eyes.

CHAPTER FIVE

Bill and Heather were not fully understanding what was taking place—they have become part of something that is totally mysterious and baffling and need some sort of intervention by an expert in this type of phenomenon. They haven't gotten to the point of reaching this conclusion, but will very soon.

Tom and Hazel had discussed a fitting compensation for Bill once they realized what he has been doing for the past twenty or so years and that he has a little girl and that Bill's mother is living with them.

"You know, darling," said Hazel to her only child, "I would truly like to meet Bill's little girl and his mother. If only he had brought them with him today."

"Yes, Mother, that would've been a wonderful thing, but maybe we can encourage Bill to let us meet them soon," acknowledged Tom to his mother.

"Dear, do you think that our offer of our family's appreciation to Bill is enough, or should we increase it in some other way as well?" said Hazel with a look of some concern about her face. "You know money is of little importance to people who have always had an abundance of the finer things in life, and none of that matters without our little Heather, so our compensation must be befitting a man like Bill for doing something so courageous. Don't you think so too, dear?"

"Mother, I would've been willing to give all that I own to save my little girl's life—just the thought of losing her terrifies me. After I lost Ruby, I thought my life was over, and Heather is certainly an irreplaceable part of her that I cling to and deeply cherish," said Tom as he looked at his mother with visions of his dearly departed wife still clear in his mind.

"The business could almost run itself with all of the fine people we have working for us, Mother, and to compensate Bill in the manner that we've already discussed will most certainly be an offer that he couldn't possibly refuse. Giving Bill a seat on our board of directors, buying out his trucking business and thereby providing him the opportunity to live a lifestyle that would afford him the ability stay home with his little girl Victoria is a generous offer, don't you agree, Mother?" said Tom.

"Yes, dear. We must formally meet her and Bill's mother as well… uh her name is Carrie I believe. We must find something for that little girl that she likes," stated Hazel with an unwavering, stern tone in her voice. "Let's invite them over as soon as possible if that's all right with you, dear?"

"Yes, as soon as possible, I agree!" affirmed Bill.

Now the plan was set in motion that will alter Bill's life and those of his little girl, Bill's mother, and also Heather in ways that will bring wonderful and amazing happiness to so many lives—thanks to a horrible accident, a kind-hearted man, and a "highway whispering" on a night that activated one of the mysteries of the universe.

Back in the room where Heather and Bill are trying to make sense of what they're discovering, Bill tells Heather about the funeral of his late wife, Tina.

"I remember holding Tori in my arms, tears rolling uncontrollably down my face, and my little girl was crying too. So many flowers, so many people attended that day. A bright blue sky with the sun shining so brightly, but it was one of the darkest days of my life. Tina left home that day to go visit a friend in the hospital. She never knew that she would never come back home to us. A drunk driver crossed the center line and hit her car head-on, killing her instantly. The guy that killed my wife…" Bill pauses, takes a deep breath as tears start filling his eyes. "…wasn't even hurt. He was sentenced to 15 years in prison for taking my wife, my life and my little girls mother from our—" Bill fights back the tears, clears his throat. "—lives."

Heather walks over to Bill and embraces him in a way that she has never held another man with the exception of her own father. Compassion, caring, understanding the pain of another human being are feelings that Heather has experienced in her life before. Losing her own mother and watching her father grieve since she died are experiences that she remembers as she holds Bill. "It's all right, Bill, I truly understand, it's all right," says Heather to this man who one wouldn't think would ever show an emotional side like this to a total stranger.

"I'm sorry, Heather. I haven't felt these feelings in a long time. I try to compartmentalize my pain of losing my wife. I have my little girl to raise and my mother to take care of." he paused briefly and then continued.

"I've worked hard all my life and struggled to provide for them, staying gone for weeks on end just to make a living. Tori—that's my little girl's name," he says with a smile, "—she wants me to find something else to do for a living but I don't know what I could do that would pay me the same just to stay home and watch my little girl grow up, attend her little school functions, you know what I mean," Bill says, opening up his heart and inner most thoughts to Heather, "don't you?

"Tori's wanted a little puppy for so long, and I want her to have one, but I've been reluctant because I feel that I need to be home all the time to help her train it, and for her to be a responsible pet owner. I realize that I need another type of job, one where I can stay at home," says Bill as he regains his composure.

Heather can sense the frustration that Bill is experiencing. "My father might be able to help you with that situation, Bill, he has holdings in many countries with our family business, Daykin Industries. My grandfather founded it long before I was born in England. When my grandfather died, my dad took control of the business and it's grown so huge that he can spend whatever time he wants here or over in the old country," she continues.

"I've lived a very good life, Bill, not to boast. I'm not one to go around and show off my family's good fortune. Instead, I realize that I'm blessed. I can inquire with my father if there's something he can help you with that will enable you to stay home more," says Heather to Bill, not knowing all the while that her father and grandmother have already made that possible for Bill if only he accepts their generous offer.

Heather thinks about her many Siberian Huskies that she owns and remembers that one is about to have puppies. "Bill, do you think your little girl would like one of my Siberian Husky puppies, uh, I think in about another week they'll be born and in another five weeks she could have the pick of the litter?" asked Heather.

"Are you kidding—you would do that for my little girl? She and I have driven out to your place before and just sit and watch your horses and dogs run and play and that's when Tori decided she wanted a Siberian Husky more that any other breed of dog, and now you're willing to just give her such an expensive dog just like that. Are you serious?" said Bill in amazement.

"Of course I'm serious." She laughs and says, "I just know Tori would love to come over and pick the one she wants, so tell her that when the time comes she can have her choice—all right?" said Heather as she smiled and felt warm inside at the thought that this small deed would bring such joy to Bill's little girl.

"I'm so excited about this I can hardly wait to see the expression on her face. Tell her she can call me anytime and also she can come over and visit and spend time here and play with the dogs and get to know them especially the one that's going to have the puppies. Her name is Sky. I named her that because she has sky-blue eyes, just like the color of your eyes, Bill," said Heather as she peered into Bill's eyes.

Bill's face turned red as he realized that Heather was the first woman who's mentioned his eyes since his late wife many years ago, back when they were dating.

These two individuals felt more and more comfortable with each other as time passed, as though they've known each other for years rather than weeks.

Bill left for his own home that day feeling that some things have changed in his life, and he hasn't yet realized what amazing changes were in store for him and his little girl, his mother, Heather and many others that they have yet to meet.

The Highways were whispering!

CHAPTER SIX

Bill arrived back at his home and could hardly wait to tell his little girl that she would soon be able to have a little puppy. He drove into the driveway, and Tori ran up to greet her dad. "Hi, Daddy. How's Heather doing?" asked Tori.

"She's fine, sweetheart, and do I have some good news to tell you about something that you've been wanting for a long time!" said Bill with a beaming smile.

Tori had a bit of a puzzled look about her little face as she looked up at her dad's smile.

"Hmmm, ah, I've been wanting a, ah, dog, but that's not it, is it, Daddy?" said Tori as she was so much wanting it to be a dog that she could almost burst with excitement at the thought of it if it were.

Bill knew that this news was going to bring such happiness to his little girl that he was also about to burst with excitement. "Baby, Heather wants you to"—Tori starts smiling clasping her hands and starts to almost jump in place with anticipation—"have the pick of the litter of one of her Siberian Huskies which is about to deliver any time now!"

Bill hardly got the words out of his mouth before Tori starts yelling, jumping up and down, screaming with such excitement and joy. She's yelling over and over, "Yes, Yes, Yes!"

"Grandmother, grandmother, grandmother!" yells Tori as she runs into the house, wanting to tell her grandmother the good news. Bill was so very happy that she was finally going to get a puppy. He felt that she was going to be responsible enough to own a pet, and it is very important to him that a person who owns a pet truly will take care of one.

Tori finds her grandmother in the kitchen. Carrie was wondering what all the excitement was about as she heard Tori yelling all through the house.

"I'm getting a puppy, I'm getting a puppy!" she tells her grandmother, laughing and almost crying at the same time.

"Whooa, little lady," said Carrie as Tori ran into the kitchen where she was watering some flowers. "What's all the excitement about?"

"I'm getting a puppy and not just any puppy. I'm getting the pick of the litter of a Siberian Husky. Heather told Dad that I could have my pick of a puppy when the mother has her puppies here really, really soon, and that I could go out there and visit them and stuff!" said Tori, almost out of breath.

Bill walked into the kitchen where his little girl and his mother were, and he was so happy for his daughter, happy that something so very, very good would come out of such a tragic event that almost cost another her life. He never realized just how much Tori wanted a pet, and now the time couldn't be more perfect for her as he felt that she would be a very good pet owner.

After losing his wife many years ago and struggling to keep working with all the pain of losing her in that accident, Bill had a little girl and his own mother to focus on; those two special people in his life were the main reason that he didn't give up. They depended on him, and he had to be strong and continue on.

Tori walked over to her dad and gave him a big hug, throwing her little arms around his waist and squeezing tightly. "Thank you, thank you, thank you!" exclaimed Tori.

Carrie, being the caring and loving mother and grandmother that she is, spoke up and said, "How about something to eat, you guys, how does a sandwich sound, maybe ham and cheese or turkey and cheese?"

Bill said, "I'm not hungry, Mom, but I'll have a glass of milk. What do you want, sweetheart?" as he looked over at Tori.

"Turkey and cheese, please, and I'll have a glass of chocolate milk. I'll get the chocolate from the fridge," said Tori, and eventually they settled down around the kitchen table, eating, laughing and spending quality time as a little family.

Heather walked out to where the dogs were housed, and they all started barking as they were well acquainted with her and knew that she would spend time with each of them, especially Sky, the one that would soon have puppies.

"Hi, girl. How are you today? Looks like it won't be long now." She petted Sky, and all the dogs were jumping and wagging their tails because they sensed that Heather would feed and give them water as she often did.

Heather loved her prized Huskies, and they clearly loved her. She has had many of these since she was a little girl herself, and they have pretty much grown up together.

I just know that Tori will be so excited to know that she'll get her choice of the puppies when they arrive soon, thought Heather as she grabbed the scoop and plunged it into the enormous bag of dry dog food and then poured it into the many bowls with waiting four-legged friends.

She walked over and closed the gate behind her, then stood there for a moment and watched them eat. It had been a long day filled with excitement, and she was feeling very tired and weak as she had not completely recovered from her accident and still had a cast on her healing broken arm.

Hazel was standing out on the back deck smoking a cigarette with her trademark cigarette holder that made the whole thing seem like it was a foot long. She saw her granddaughter walking towards her and could tell that she was tired from the way Heather was walking.

When she got a little closer Hazel said, "Dear, are you all right? I think maybe you should sit and rest for a bit or maybe lie down. It hasn't been that long since your accident, and you haven't fully recovered, so come on inside." Hazel put out the cigarette, put the holder in her pocket, and reached for Heather's arm. They walked inside and up the stairs into Heather's bedroom.

Hazel reached over and pulled back the covers while Heather undressed, slipped into her pajamas and then climbed into her bed ever so slowly. "Thanks Nana, I love you," said Heather, with a weakened voice that was almost inaudible. "Nana, please stop smoking. I love you and couldn't bear to lose you." Then this tired young lady quickly drifted off to sleep.

Hazel reached over and pulled the hair back away from her beloved granddaughter and thought to herself that she really did need to quit smoking, but she enjoyed it. Then she walked out of the room and slowly closed her door.

Heather drifted off into a deep, deep sleep within seconds of closing her eyes. A light shone at the end of a dark tunnel as Heather seemed to float towards the light, and in this light was the silhouette of a person standing there. The closer she got to the light, the more easily she could tell that it was a young lady holding out her hand towards Heather, whispering to Heather something that she couldn't make out until she drifted closer to this spirit.

Heather. You must help me. You must help us all. Pleeease! said this beautiful, ghostly spirit that Heather recognized; she felt a warm comfort as this lady spirit made herself known to Heather as the late wife of Bill. *I am Tina Wilson, and I need your help!*

Instantly, Heather awakened from this mysterious vision she had just seen in her sleep. It seemed as though she had just lain down, but several hours had passed while she lay there dreaming—or was it a dream?

She looked over and could tell that she had truly been asleep for several hours. Climbed out of bed and walking into her bathroom, she took off her pajamas and stepped into the shower. She turned on the warm water, and soon the steam had fogged up the shower door. Reaching out she took the shampoo and poured it into her wet, silky brown hair, lathering it all over and then rinsing it. As the steam cleared for an instant she glanced at the door and saw words appear, slowly written by an invisible hand. *"Pleeease help us Heather—you must help uusssss!"* The spirits were reaching out to her now, but it didn't frighten Heather at all; in fact she felt comforted with what she had witnessed.

Finishing her shower, she slipped on some clothes. She walked over to the bureau, grabbed her phone, and dialed Bill's number. One ring, two rings, three, and then she heard "Hello." It was Tori who answered her daddy's phone.

Heather smiled as she said, "Hello, this is Heather. Are you Victoria?"

"Yes. How are you doing? I hope you're getting better since your accident." said Tori as she was smiling too.

"Daddy told me about the puppy that you want to give to me. Thank you sooooo much, Ms. Heather. I'm so excited. Thank you!" said Tori with such excitement ringing through her little voice.

"You can come over anytime you like to visit and meet Sky, the mother that will soon have the puppies. I can't wait to meet you too, Tori, or should I call you Victoria?" asked Heather as to be polite to this little lady who might want a stranger to call her by her full name.

"Oh, you can call me Tori. All my friends call me Tori," said Tori.

"Well, all right then, but only if you call me Heather and not Ms. Heather—okay?" said Heather to this polite little girl.

"Can I speak with your dad, please? I hope I'm not interrupting you guys, am I?" said Heather, almost apologizing.

"Oh no, not at all, Heather, I'll go get him. He's outside working on something." said Tori as she ran out of the house with phone in hand yelling, "Daaaddy—Daaaaddy telephone." Running up to her dad, she handed him the phone saying, "It's Heather," with a big smile directed towards her dad.

"Hello, Heather, how are you?" He motioned for his smiling little girl to run along while he talked with Heather.

"I'm fine, Bill. Sorry I interrupted what you were doing. I have to tell you what happened to me a short while ago."

"Are you sure everything's all right, Heather? You sound like something's wrong," stated Bill, sensing that something was indeed wrong.

"I wasn't feeling well, so I went upstairs and went to bed. I was so tired and weak that I couldn't stay up any longer. I woke up and took a hot shower and was shampooing my hair and just happened to glance over at the shower door and saw words starting to appear on the door as though a spirit was writing them," explained Heather, hoping that Bill wouldn't think she was losing her mind.

Bill, not knowing how to respond to such a statement, didn't say a word. He was totally speechless, which created a long pause, and it made Heather feel a little uneasy at even mentioning it in the first place.

"Bill, please believe me. I'm not making this up. I think I know what might be happening to me. We need to talk about it, because I think your late wife and other people that I've seen while in the coma and what just happened in the shower are signs that they're trying to communicate with me, with us for a reason, and I don't know what to do!" said Heather.

CHAPTER SEVEN

Now the events were starting to unfold as to the dreams and visions of people, or one might say *spirits*—the voices of souls who need the living to communicate with for some unknown reason.

Bill knows that Heather is telling the truth, but finds the truth hard to believe. Who would believe a story like she just told him, and why would his late wife be trying to communicate with him?

Bill, Tori, Heather, Carrie, Tom, Hazel, and all the others—including a puppy—will pull you deeper into a mystery with each turn of the page.

Bill calmly tells Heather that they should meet somewhere and discuss the many things that seem to be bringing these two individuals together for some unknown reason.

They decide to meet back at Heather's place and that Bill should bring Tori along with him to visit the mother, Sky, of her soon-to-be first-ever puppy.

Bill walks through the house looking for his little girl and finds his mother in the living room holding a picture of her late husband. Bill walks over to her, puts his arm around this person who gave him life, and tells her, "Mom, I love you. Are you all right?" Bill knows that his mother truly misses her late husband, Alexander.

"Yes, dear, I'm fine. I just miss your dad. Can I fix you something to eat or drink, son?" she says.

"No. I'm looking for Tori, have you seen her?" he says.

"I think she's in the attic playing. She likes going up there and looking at some of the things that were her mother's," she tells her son as she puts the picture of her husband back on the table.

"Thanks, Mom. I miss Dad too!" He gives her a hug and kiss on the cheek and walks away to find his little girl.

Bill goes upstairs and walks into the part of his house that he has seldom gone into, especially since his wife died. He looks over in a corner where some boxes and a large trunk are sitting with their lids open and finds Tori sitting there with a dress that was once her mother's.

"Hi, baby," he says as he sits down next to her and snuggles up close and puts his arm around his baby girl.

Tori looks at her dad and says, "My mother use to wear this, didn't she?"

"Yes, honey, she did, and I just know that she'd be glad that you're here thinking about her now." Bill reaches over and touches the dress that his late wife wore on their wedding day.

White satin with lots of lace. Bill thinks back on that special day many years ago, the day that was one of the happiest he can ever recall, with the exception of the day that his precious Tori was born.

"Say, sweetheart. I spoke with Heather a few minutes ago, and I've got to go over there for awhile. I was wondering if perhaps you would like to go too. Heather said that you could come over and spend some time with the dogs—that's if you want to?" he said, knowing full well that she would love that so very, very much.

"Oh Daddy, can I? Do you mind?" she said as she placed her mother's dress back in the trunk with such gentleness and respect and then closed the lid.

"Sure, let's go." He stood-up and helped Tori to her feet.

Down the stairs they went, looking for Carrie, who was gazing out the front window.

"Mom, Tori and I are going over to Heather's for a little visit, please come with us and get out of the house for awhile all right? It will do you good to go with us," said Bill, knowing that his mother was feeling a little depressed. "I won't take no for an answer!"

"Well, I guess it wouldn't hurt to go, and yes, it will do me some good. You know I've never been to that big house before. I would really like to see it up close. You don't think they would mind, do you, dear?" said Carrie with a bit of apprehension in her voice.

"It'll be all right, Mom. They are truly wonderful people and are so hospitable. Besides, Tori gets to visit with the dog that's going to have a litter of puppies soon. Tori gets to have the pick of the litter," stated a reassuring son.

They all loaded into the truck, and off they went on their little adventure. Meanwhile on the other side of town, down in the valley, Heather was preparing herself for this visit. She had gotten ready and informed her father and grandmother that they would be having Bill and Tori over.

Tom told his mother, "Mother, I think when they get here we should tell Bill about our intentions of having him becoming a board member and also that other thing we discussed."

"Dear, I believe you're right. We should tell him now rather than wait any longer. I need to go ahead and step down from the board so that he can assume my place there."

Heather was fully aware of what her father and Nana were planning for Bill when he and Tori arrived. The excitement of Bill returning and also that he would be bringing his little girl with him only added to that excitement.

They drove past the cross that Bill placed alongside the road where his beloved wife died so horribly seven years earlier. Bill always says, "I love you, baby!" as they pass the little memorial and Tori always says, "I love you, Mommy!"

I love you, tooooo! whispered the spirit of Tina as they continued on their journey, getting closer each day to unraveling this mystery.

This little family of three finally arrived at their new friends' home, and they were welcomed with opened arms. The Shylers weren't the type to let their wealth blind them to what is truly important in life.

They have all lost loved ones, both the Shylers and the Wilsons, and now they were together for the first time ever, setting the scene for their life-altering events that have already started to take place.

The Wilsons were taken into a large room with food, drinks, and some gifts for Tori. Bill also had a couple of gifts, and he was to have to wait a little while longer to find what they were even though he had no idea he was to receive anything at all.

Tori's gifts were in the form of pet supplies for her soon-to-be new puppy, like puppy food, a grooming brush, shampoo, a collar, and other assorted doggy items.

"Are all of these things for me?" said a most excited little girl who could hardly believe this was actually happening.

"They certainly are yours, dear. Also, soon you'll have the puppy to go along with these things," said Hazel, who remembered Heather as a little girl like Tori when her granddaughter was ten years old. It really warmed Hazel's heart to watch this little person.

Heather asked Tori if she would like to go outside and visit Sky—the mother of the soon-to-be puppies.

"Oh, can I please, Heather? I can't believe this, Daddy," said Tori with a smile from ear to ear.

"Let's go outside," said Heather, and off they went.

Hazel paired off with Carrie, and they went outside on the deck for tea and conversation. Once there, Hazel reached into her left pocket. She pulled out her cigarette holder, placed a cigarette in it, and then asked if Carrie minded.

"Of course not. Please do. You know when I was younger I smoked one and it made me ill and I never did that again," said Carrie as she looked at all the beautiful plants and flowers around about and scanned the whole area and all its massiveness.

Hazel lit the cigarette at once and began to smoke. "Carrie, my son and I are planning on telling Bill something—in fact he may be telling him at this very moment. I wanted to get you off to ourselves and tell you that it is an offer of something from our family to yours. Call it appreciation for what your son did when he saved our Heather. Please understand that she is everything to us and what Bill did that horrible night—well—we are very appreciative.

"Let me try and explain our offer." Hazel started telling Carrie what it was that would change their lives forever more. Carrie's eyes instantly widened, and she leaned back into her chair and placed her hand over her mouth as to keep herself from screaming with utter amazement.

Meanwhile, back in the room where Bill and Tom were, Tom asked Bill some questions about his trucking business and what it was that he wanted in his life more than anything else.

"Well—" There was a long pause. "—I want more than anything else, to be able to spend more time with my little girl and my mom, after all, they're all I have left since my wife died seven years ago," said Bill as he looked at Tom, who was sitting across from him in a comfortable-looking leather chair.

"I've worked hard all my life, and the trucking business is all that I know. I started out working for someone else and realized that I could earn more if I owned my own equipment, so I bought an old truck and trailer from a friend of mine who wanted to retire and started on my own," stated Bill as he reflected back over his life.

"Bill, my mother and I own and operate a very successful business that my late father founded long before I was born. When he died, I eventually took control, and I am the chairman of the board, and my mother is a major shareholder. Mother is getting to that point in her life that she wants to retire completely from our business—hence, she will relinquish her position on the board of directors.

"That position pays her an annual salary of three hundred fifty thousand dollars per year, and the shares she holds are worth in the millions. Mother and I are offering you her position on the board, and she will transfer her shares to you—thus creating a way for you to spend more time with your family while you pursue a life that is still within the trucking industry but from the other side of the steering wheel, so to speak.

"Bill, we truly need you, your experience, your good business sense, and more importantly your high level of values and thoughtfulness regarding family. You see, my family is all that I have as well Bill, and if I had lost Heather that night you just happened to drive by, and you hadn't stopped, then my life would have stopped then also. I know that you love your family and your late wife, and I love my family and also my late wife, so you see—we have more in common than one might think. I, or I should say we, need you in our lives and in our business. Giving you this tremendous opportunity is not charity—no, no, Bill—this is with the deepest gratitude and love from our family to yours. So here is the ability for you to stay with your family and watch your little girl grow as I have been able to watch mine grow and spend more time with your mother, who I'm quite certain would like to have her only son around more instead of out of state most of the time." Tom continued speaking with Bill, who was taken aback by this great, great generosity. They continued for several hours, talking and planning, and Bill would just shake his head, not fully understanding why this wonderful good fortune would come his way in life.

Heather had taken Tori out to the pen where the dogs were kept, and Sky took to Tori immediately as did all the other dogs. Yes, Tori was right where she wanted to be, laughing and playing with these wonderful Siberian Huskies as Heather watched.

Heather could almost see herself as a young girl like Tori when she was her age, laughing and playing. After all, isn't that what children do?

"Tori, have you thought of a name for your puppy when it's born?" asked Heather.

"Oh yes, I want a little girl puppy, and I'll name her Terra. You don't mind if I have a girl puppy, do you Heather?" asked Tori with a bit of reservation in her voice.

"Sweetie, you can have whichever one you choose," replied Heather.

Meanwhile, back on the deck where Hazel and Carrie were, they had come to realize that they also had much in common. Their love of the outdoors and their knowledge of plants and flowers were almost on equal footing. Also, their love of family was the most important part of their lives.

Hazel had already started telling her new friend Carrie about the plans that she and Tom were offering Bill, plans that would completely change their lives. The utter weight of what they were willing to just give was breathtaking and awe-inspiring, and it took Carrie completely by surprise, so much so that she had to sit for a while just to let it settle in her thought processes.

Bill was finally persuaded by Tom, who was by all rights a true salesman and leader of many. He had run his late father's business with a keen business sense and understanding of what others' needs and wants were: the pride one gets in working at a job and getting paid a good wage for a hard day's work.

Bill and Tom shook hands in agreement, and the deal was settled with all but the required paperwork and signatures, and of course that would come later with a short trip to England where the headquarters was. Bill would be introduced to the other board members and would meet some of the workers and senior drivers that work for Daykin Industries.

Much had to be done, mostly paperwork, and that would not take more than a week overseas, and then Bill could come back to his hometown with a different outlook on life.

Bill took his leave from Tom and went to where his little girl and Heather were with the many dogs. As he approached, he saw a very happy little girl who was in tall cotton (a Southern saying meaning happy or very pleased).

Heather saw Bill and walked towards him. She smiled, knowing that he and her father had talked and what the offer to Bill was. She felt that all was well with Bill and that he had accepted her father's most generous offer, as he was smiling such a smile that his eyes were just slits, only opened enough to be able to see what was in front of him.

"You knew what was going to happen when we arrived today, didn't you?" said Bill as he looked at her, still shaking his head no—in complete disbelief.

"Yes, I confess. I've known from the time they started planning on telling you. I gather you agreed?" she asked as she looked up into what little bit of blue eyes she could see.

"Yes. Your father is a very convincing man and wouldn't take no for an answer. I really can't believe all that's happened, Heather. I mean all I did was stop and pull you from your car that night." he said.

"Now Bill, can we talk about the other thing. The spirits? I, ah, think that they're trying to tell me or us something, and I don't know what to do or who to turn to for advice. Are there people who deal with this sort of thing and how do we find one to tell us what to do?" she said as she glanced around to keep an eye on Tori.

"I guess we can look on the Internet or look in the phone book. Do you know any of the professor's at your school that might know a person that deals in the 'paranormal'? Maybe they could help," said Bill.

"We can go and visit Steve on campus. He's one of my professors. I must let you know, though, that he likes me as more than just a student. He might be able to help us because he's a professor of psychology—dealing with behavior management. If he can't help us then I'm quite certain he can direct us to someone who might," Heather told Bill.

"Daddy, look. This is Sky. She's going to have puppies soon, and I can have one!" said his joyful daughter, who couldn't possibly be happier.

"I see, baby." He looked at his precious little girl playing with man's best friend.

Heather told Bill that she would call Steve at school and talk with him and see if he could possibly help them with finding out about the occult, the spirit world of those who have departed the living world and haven't gone on to the next life.

The day was filled with much happiness for both families. Bill, Tori, and Carrie were Tom, Heather, and Hazel were helping their new friends in ways that many simply just dream about.

Bill and Heather finally ended up on the back deck which overlooked the whole area, including that part where Tori was still with the dogs. Heather picked up the phone and called Steve at his campus office; he had his calls forwarded to his cell phone.

The phone rang several times and then she heard on the other end "Hello, Heather, how are you feeling?" said the cocky academia.

As soon as she heard him say that, she knew he had caller ID, and replied with, "Hello Professor. I'm doing much better, thank you. My arm is healing and should get the cast off in a few more days. Other than that, I am doing great." Heather knew that he was going to come out with some come-on line to her.

"Heather, when are you going to let me take you out to dinner? I mean we have known each other for what—uh—three, four years now, and each time I ask you out you always have an excuse of some kind," said the arrogant and full-of-himself teacher.

"Well, Professor—"

He interrupted. "Call me Steve. Please. You don't have to be so formal," he said, pressing Heather to do something she really didn't want to do.

"Steve, Bill, the man who saved my life, is here with me now and we both need to speak with you on a professional level about something. Can we meet you somewhere today, as soon as possible?" said Heather, getting control of the conversation and heading it into the area she had called about, not about what Steve obviously wants.

"Oh, I see. That man is there with you now—uh—Bill is his name. Yes, well, uh—yes. Of course, Heather. I can see you both. I'm in town now, and if you two would like to meet me at the coffee house, then I can see you in about half an hour, if that's all right?" he said as if he realized that now wasn't the time to try and put the make on her. Heather had tactfully forced him to put on his professional face.

"Yes, certainly. We can meet you there. Half an hour. Thanks, Professor. I—uh—we really do appreciate this!" She ended the call, smiled at Bill, and then said, "Can we take Tori with us, Bill, or should she stay here?"

"I can ask Mom to keep an eye on her. After all, Tori is having the time of her life, and I know she won't mind staying here awhile longer!" said Bill.

Heather and Bill okay that with Carrie and Hazel, and of course all was fine, so off they went in Bill's truck.

Out onto Highway 69 they drove. The windows were down, and soon they were approaching the area where Bill's late wife died and the cross was. Bill slowed down and said, "I love you, baby."

Heather looked more closely at the cross this time, because the lady who died there many years ago was communicating with her for some unknown reason.

They drove slowly past the accident site where Bill stopped that night. He thought to himself that Heather was lucky that she lived, and he felt good that he didn't have to drive past another cross where someone else died. He looked over at Heather with her beautiful long hair blowing in the wind as she gazed at the site where she could have easily died that night.

Heather turned around and saw Bill looking at her. She smiled, reached over, put her hand gently on Bill's right hand, and said, "Thank you for saving me that night!"

"It's all right, you're all right, and that's what's important, Heather." Bill gently pulled his hand away from Heather's and placed it on the steering wheel. He knew that she was grateful for what he had done, but he felt like he was betraying his late wife when she placed her hand on his as they drove past the memorial where Tina died.

Bill has never dated or befriended another female since Tina died and for him to be alone with another woman, especially one so beautiful, and to have that woman put her hand gently on Bill's, well—he felt a little guilty for some reason, as though he was betraying his love for his late wife.

Heather could tell that Bill was nervous when she touched him that way and she truly didn't mean anything other than she was grateful and felt like he was her "knight in shining armor," so to speak. After all, he did rescue her.

CHAPTER EIGHT

They drove on past the accident site and both looked, and they both thought of that horrific night. Soon the truck pulled up in front of the coffee shop, and they walked in and found Steve sitting over in the back corner.

"Hi, Steve. How are you doing?" said Heather.

"I'm fine, girl, how's your arm?" Steve spoke as though he and Heather had a thing going on.

"Oh, it's all right. I'll get the cast off soon."

"Steve, I'd like to introduce you to Bill—Bill Wilson," she said with some trepidation.

Bill put his hand out to shake Steve's, but only received a grip kind of like a dead fish. Not much of a manly grip.

"Hello, I'm certainly glad to meet you uh—Bill." Steve pulled his hand out of Bill's strong, masculine grip, feeling like he had just removed it from a vice.

"Good to meet you, Steve," said Bill.

They sat down and started some small talk, then progressed to the purpose of the visit.

"Steve, how would a person communicate with the departed?" asked Heather.

"I haven't got a clue," said Steve after a long pause. There was a puzzled look on her professor's face.

"Is that what you wanted to talk with me about?" he said.

"I thought you wanted me to tell you something relating to my professional credentials and expertise. I would have never guessed you would want me to tell you about the spirit world. I really haven't got any idea at all," he said, as though they had just wasted his time.

Heather could sense that Bill had become a little agitated at Steve's seeming lack of interest.

"This is a serious request, Professor, and if you don't have a clue… well, can you at least point us in the right direction?" said a mildly upset Heather.

"I suppose one could either check the yellow pages of the phone book or go on-line and search for a spiritual or mystic adviser or something of that sort. When do you think you'll be coming back to class?" said the teacher.

"I may just withdraw for the remainder of the year. I don't think I can get through all the back homework, missed tests and such, so I'll just withdraw for the remainder of the year," she said.

"Oh you don't need to do that, Heather, I can work with you—uh—" And then he realized that Bill was there, cleared his throat, and continued, "—well, maybe that would be a good idea. Yes, I think you should do that and maybe start the new year off all anew," he said.

Bill could tell this idiot was trying to put the make on her right there in front of him, but kept his composure and didn't say a word; after all, she had no romantic connection to Bill.

He and Heather stood up, politely said good-bye, and left. Once outside they both kind of laughed, and Heather said, "Can you believe the nerve of him?"

They then got back into the truck and drove down the street. Bill turned down a street that he doesn't ever remember going down before and Heather said, "STOP THE TRUCK!" and his foot hit the brake, not knowing what had happened.

"What's wrong!" said Bill.

Heather looked at Bill, and she then pointed over to her right—directing him to look at a sign that read KENDARI'S PALM READING & MYSTIC ADVISING.

"Can you believe that—I mean—I—uh?" she said.

"I've never been down this street before, I don't understand why I turned right instead of left. It's almost like the truck turned on it's own—like—uh—this is getting weird, Heather," he said.

It's me, darling—it's all of us drawing you both to help us. Soon you'll figure it oooouuuuttt, said Bills' late wife. She (Tina) and the other spirits were guiding these unsuspecting people in the direction they wanted them to go.

Bill parked the truck, and they both got out, walked to the front door, and paused. They were so uncertain and reluctant to go further but yet drawn to go forward with their quest.

Heather reached out her right hand and knocked loudly—once, twice, three, and almost a fourth—then suddenly the door opened with a squeak, slowly revealing the occupant within: a small, unassuming woman with a slight limp. This lady used a cane that seemed as though it were an extension of her arm.

"What can I do for ya?" she said.

"We're wanting to speak with Kendari please. Are you uh—?"

"Yep—that would be me," she said with a smile.

"Come on inside, please excuse my house. My cat lies everywhere, and I'm not the tidiest person in town," she said as she led these two persons into her parlor.

The three walked into the room that was dark—much like one might have seen in a movie. Dark curtains, dark painted walls, creaky hardwood floors, and candles burning throughout.

"Have a seat. I believe I know what you want from me." She looked over in the direction of Bill.

Heather looked at Bill, he looked at her, and they both looked at Kendari. *Had they gone too far with this whole thing, had they stepped into something that they might regret in the attempt to find what was causing their lives to become something more than either ever wanted or dreamed? They will get their answers to these questions and more—-very very soon.*

"Heather, when you walked into my home, and you too, Bill—I felt a surge of energy flowing from you both, the likes of which I haven't experienced in many, many years," she said as she pulled the hair away from her bad eye and tucked the unkempt locks behind her ears.

"I, uh…haven't even told you what we're hear for," said Heather as she turned and looked over at her partner across from her.

"I felt the energy flowing around you more than him, but certainly you have a lot going on with you, girl—WOW—you're hot with energy—glowing with a blue hue of spirits circling you. He has a lot going on with the spirits too, but you, girl—what have you done to get these ghosts wanting to be around you so much?" Kendari said as she shook her head and then lit another candle as one near her had gone out.

"I really don't know for sure, but I was in a terrible accident not very long ago and was in a coma for awhile. The spirits started making themselves known to me during that time. One even came to me and wrote on the shower door the other day when I was taking a hot shower."

"It was his late wife that wrote on the door—Tina—wasn't it?" said Kendari as she looked at Bill with a warm smile.

"Yes—oh yes—it was her," said Heather with amazement at this strange person who seemed to know many things and yet she had only just met these two people.

Bill had a somewhat puzzled look on his face, not understanding fully the scope and depth of mysterious events that seems to be taking place more and more frequently.

Meanwhile, back at the Shyler estate, Tori was having the time of her little life with all the dogs and of course looking at the horses running all over the pasture, seemingly putting on a show just for this little animal lover.

Hazel and Carrie felt so comfortable with each other, as though they had known one another for most of their lives. Hazel opened up with her heartfelt feelings about the loss of her dearly beloved husband, with the story of how they met, fell in love and married, and with how she ended up living part of the time in Hayti, Missouri.

Likewise, Carrie told the story of her late husband, his death, the birth of their son—Bill—and how they've grown closer than ever, living under the same roof, with Carrie taking care of her little granddaughter.

The minutes turned to hours as the sky started closing its eyes, with darkness creeping up on a most interesting day.

Bill and Heather talked with Kendari about their lives, the accident, the mysterious visions of spirits which have manifested themselves more and more with each passing day.

Kendari had become Bill and Heather's link to the spirits, and they set up a time when they could all start unraveling these mysteriously strange happenings.

Bill asked Kendari how it was that she was able to see these ghosts when they could not—with the exception of Bill's one time when he rescued Heather.

"I was also in an accident when I was a little girl at home. I was playing in the back yard with some friends, running, and I ran into a low-hanging tree branch. It put me in the hospital, and I lost my eye. I remember the pain was for an instant, but I was in a coma for several weeks. It was while in the coma that I started having spirits come to visit me—I guess it's been about fifty-five years ago now," said Kendari as she adjusted her eye patch. "I was so very much afraid at first but over time they became more like friends as all the children I played with way back then stopped playing with me at the Children's home where we all lived. It was an orphanage you see…ah…I was abandoned as a baby and lived in a state-run facility until I turned eighteen, then I had to move out and find a way of life on my own. It was extremely hard for the first ten or so years but got a little better after that. Ah—let's get together again and start getting to the bottom of these spirits desires. Can you two meet me back here day after tomorrow—say about twelve noon?"

"Of course we can—ah—I mean ah—Bill, I'm sorry—can you too?" said Heather not thinking that Bill might have prior plans.

"Sure, certainly—I can make the time, and we'll meet you back here then."

Kendari walked these two caretakers of untold mysteries to her front door and watched as they drove off. She then closed the door, and several of these spirits, including Bills' late wife, Tina, told her, *THANNNK YOUUUU FORR HHELLPPPINNGG UUSSSSsssssssss.*

Bill and Heather were excited at the day's events as they drove back to Heather's place, and they talked about many things and were becoming closer and closer and more comfortable with each other as though they had known each other far longer than they really had.

Tori had played with the animals to her heart's content and was filled up with the love a child has for pets. Sky—the mother of the soon-to-be puppies—was close to giving birth to this litter, and Sky sensed that this little girl would end up with one of her precious litter and was at ease with this gift that she would give to this girl named Tori.

CHAPTER NINE

Bill and Heather arrived back at the vast Shyler estate and walked into the back yard where Tori was wrapped up in having fun with the dogs and the two matriarchs were still in deep conversation.

"Hi, Mom. Are you and Tori about ready to head back home?" said Bill.

"I suppose so, dear. Oh Tori, come on, sweetheart, time to go home," said Carrie as she looked at her son and then over in the direction of her granddaughter.

"Bye-bye, guys. I'll see you all again soon—at least I hope it'll be soon," said Tori as she ran to greet her dad and Heather.

"Did you two do what you needed to get done today?" Hazel said as she glanced over her granddaughter and Bill.

"Well…ah…I guess you could say that we're further down that road than we were before we left this morning. We met the most interesting person today. A lady that will most certainly add a little spice to all that's been happening so far," said Heather with a look of confidence.

Bill hugged his little girl as though they hadn't seen each other in weeks. "I love you, baby." Bill picked up Tori and held her close.

Heather smiled at this display of affection.

Carrie and Hazel said their goodbyes, and they all walked out to bid each other good night.

******

What a day this has been for all parties involved—including the spirits who have helped guide events and people in the direction they so desperately need them to go.

Bill, Carrie, and Tori all drove back home and discussed all that they had done that day. Tori was completely beside herself even as they drove home; she couldn't believe that she would soon have a dog of her own, and not just any dog, but a Siberian Husky.

Carrie told her son and granddaughter (when she could find a break in Tori's conversation about the animals, that is), she had missed having something in common with another, as that was what drew her and her new friend—Hazel—so close together. Carrie missed that when she lost her soul mate. Carrie was invited to come over anytime, and was also given Hazel's private phone number for chats at anytime.

Bill was a patient person and mainly listened to the most important women in his life, and before they knew it, they had arrived back where they had started their day.

"Oh Dad, how was your day?" asked Tori as they opened their doors to walk into the house.

"Very, very interesting!" he said with a smile.

They were almost physically drained as each just wanted to get a quick bite to eat and clean up, and then go to bed.

Kendari was also drained from her day as well. She has been re-visited by some spirits; this day it seemed as though all of them wanted to have their particular situation addressed at the same time, but that will take some time, and they know that they each must wait their turn, based on their importance and length of time in their realm.

It doesn't occur that often when a person becomes a source of understanding that the spirits can feel comfortable with making themselves known. They (the spirits) could actually make themselves known to a person but have that person be so terrified that they aren't a suitable medium or go-between for them to make their desires known, in which case the need to go through a mystic adviser, such as Kendari.

The night has fallen, darkness has consumed the land, and the spirits are a bit restless. They often get that way when they know that some of their numbers may soon be moving on to a different realm.

Little Tori is fast asleep and is visited by her late mother—Tina. She is sitting beside her little girl, smiling and thinking how much her girl has grown over the years since she died.

I LOVE YOUUU, SWEEEETTHEARTTTT, MOMMMYY LOVESSS YOUUU, BABBBBY, ANNDD SOOOONN I'LLLL BEEE MOVVINNGG ONN TOOO WHEERRE I WILLL SPENNDD

EETERNITY AANNDD WAITTT ONNN YOUU ANDDD YOURR FATHERRR TOOO JOINNN MEEEE.

And the night started to give way to the next day with the sun rising in the east.

Tina's spirit spent part of the night with her little girl, and occasionally she sat next to her husband while he slept. Bill had a dream of his late wife talking to him, as he often dreamed of her, but this time the dream was different. When he awakened from this dream, he felt as though it was time that he moved on with his life, that his wife would be all right with him possibly finding another mate.

Tina's spirit also visited the estate of the Shylers', and she specifically visited the Siberian Husky that was soon going to have puppies. Tina spoke with this mother dog and thanked her for allowing her daughter Tori to have one of her puppies. Sky, the mother dog, felt comforted at the thought that a puppy of hers would bring so much joy to a little girl.

Sky let Tina's spirit know that she would be having the puppies in a very few hours and should let Tori know this.

When Tori's eye's opened she ran downstairs, told her grandmother that Sky would be having her puppies in a little while, and asked if she could go over to watch this take place.

"Baby, let's wait until your dad comes downstairs and you can ask him, is that all right?" said Carrie as she continued making homemade biscuits and gravy from a recipe that she was given by her own mother almost fifty years earlier.

"I'll just go up and see if he's awake already." Off she went to hurry her daddy in his waking-up process.

Standing outside of his bedroom door, she put her ear to the door and listened for any sounds that might lead her to believe that he was awake. She thought she heard something, but this was really her mother's spirit assisting in this endeavor; Tina caused the wind to blow through the window, and it sounded like her dad sometimes does when he whistles.

Tori opened the door and ran over to his bedside and found him just turning over with a smile on his face, because he knew it was his little girl and she always had priority over most everything including his sleep.

"What is it, baby?" he said as he reached over and wrapped his arms and covers around his little girl, pulling her close to him and started tickling her.

Tori laughed and wiggled and squirmed as he continued to tickle her, and then he held her close, hugged and kissed her, and said, "Have you had enough or do you want some more?"

"Daddy, I love you and we need to go over to Heather's place cause Sky is going to have her puppies in a little bit."

Bill for some reason didn't question why she knew this was going to happen; he simply said, "All right, sweetheart, let me get up and get dressed. Let's eat something and I'll call Heather and ask her if it's okay with her if we come over."

Tori's smile couldn't possibly be any bigger as she hugged her dad and said "Hurry up, Daddy!" She ran downstairs and told her grandmother what they were going to do as Carrie was just about finished with making breakfast.

Bill got dressed and grabbed his phone to call Heather when the phone rang just as he was about to dial her number.

"Hello—good morning, Heather." He saw that it was her on his caller ID.

"Can you guys come over soon, because Sky is about to have her puppies and I would truly like for Tori to be here to watch, that's if you don't mind and haven't anything else to do?"

"I was just about to call you and ask if we could come over for the very same reason. Tori had this feeling that the litter would arrive soon, and I guess she was right. Sure, we'll be right over—just let us eat breakfast and we'll drive right over."

"Great—see you soon, Bill, and be careful."

Father and daughter and the cook ate breakfast, and they kissed the cook, and out to the truck they went. Bill and Tori drove past the cross where Tina died, and they both said they loved her. She was there waiting as they past. *I LOVEEE YOUUUU TOOO*, she said with a smile.

Finally arriving at the Shyler estate, Bill and Tori got out of the vehicle and walked around back and saw Heather and an attendant working with Sky. Just as they walked up to where Heather was, Sky started delivering what was to be the first of four, small, beautiful newborn puppies. The mother checked out each one as they were born and then cleaned each one while they cried. Tori was simply amazed at this wonderful event that captivated her.

Tori saw the puppy that she wanted. The second one born looked straight into Tori's eyes, and they connected as though each knew the other. Normally, newborn puppies' eyes are closed, but this time, this particular one's eyes were open.

"Can I hold mine now?" asked Tori with such impatience.

"Well, sweetie, let's give Sky a little longer to get her babies all cleaned up, and then I'm certain they'll want to eat, so maybe in a little while," Heather said, knowing the procedure from past deliveries.

Bill stood by watching this miracle take place. Seeing his daughter consumed with amazement and joy, he couldn't be happier for Tori, knowing that she actually watched the birth of her puppy.

The spirit of Tina was there as well, watching this event that she helped to create for the benefit of her little girl. She knew that her time was coming to an end in this spirit form and that she would be moving onto the next realm.

After awhile, the threesome decides to walk back to the deck and have something to eat and think about what had just happened.

"How did you guys know that Sky was about to have her puppies?" asked Heather.

"My mom comes to me sometimes in my dreams, and we talk. Mom told me that Sky would be having her puppies and for me to wake up and to wake my dad and drive over to watch, because it was very important," said Tori.

"She comes to me in my dreams, too. It bothered me at first when she started visiting but as time passed I was all right with it. I think Tina has been wanting something for a long time, and all that has happened since your accident, Heather, has been a culmination of events that's going to lead us to some conclusion," said Bill.

"Maybe we should contact Kendari and ask if we can move our next session with her forward. I have a feeling that Tina needs us for something very soon," stated Heather.

"Tori, sweetie, you have an amazing gift with the dogs and when your puppy was born, Terra looked at you as though you two already knew each other. That's spooky," said Heather as she looked at Tori with a puzzled look on her face.

"I've always gotten along with animals because they know that I like them, and they like me in return," stated Tori.

"I'll call Kendari and ask her if we can visit with her sooner than our next scheduled appointment time. I think I programmed her phone number in my phone—uh, let's see here—" Bill scrolls down through all the number's and finally finds it. "—here it is," he said as he dialed the number. One ring, two, three—

"Hello, Bill," said Kendari.

The hair stood up on Bill's arms when she answered the phone and said *Hello, Bill*.

"How, uh, did you know it was me?" he asked with a shaky tone in his voice.

"HA—I scared you, didn't I? I have caller ID on my phone." She laughed, and Bill started laughing too. Heather and Tori started laughing too, but they were only laughing because it's contagious.

"What are we laughing at, Bill?" asked Heather.

"I'll tell you later." He then gathered his composure and started to tell Kendari why he was calling, but Kendari cut him off and said, "I know why you are calling, and yes, you guys can come over now if you like and bring your little girl with you too—okay?"

"How did you know my little girl, uh, oh—never mind—uh, we'll see you in a little while and thanks," muttered Bill with a sort of puzzled voice.

"Baby, can you let your puppy go back to her mother? Then you can go with Heather and me over to this lady's place that's going to help us with some things regarding—uh…" He didn't know quite how to tell Tori what they were going to this person's house for.

Tori placed her precious little puppy ever so gently down next to the other puppies who were feeding, and Terra nosed her way into the fray and joined her brothers and sister. Bill, Heather, and Tori walked over to the truck and drove off towards town.

Heather's phone rang. She looked at the caller ID and saw that it was Adam—Heather's old flame—and she just let it go to voice-mail and then turned her phone off.

"Was it important?" asked Bill.

"No, no it wasn't important at all," she said and finally realized that it was totally over between her and Adam; she just needed to tell him soon.

This trio arrived at Kendari's home and stepped up to the front door. Bill reached out to knock, and suddenly the door opened. "Please come in," said this mysterious person.

Bill said, "How did you know that we were here?"

"I looked out the window. HA—I'm good, but not that good. I can't see through walls," said Kendari.

They all looked at each other and laughed.

"Hi, Miss Kendari," said Tori with a smile. "Are you going to help us with my mother? 'Cause she told me you were going to help us with something."

Bill put his arm around his little girl and looked over at Heather. "Baby, this lady is going to help us, yes."

"Please come inside, into my parlor. I believe that the time has come to help Tina into the next realm. She has guided the events that led to this moment. This coming together, if you will, of strangers whose lives will never be the same after today."

"Please have a seat and I will close these curtains." Kendari walked over to the window and closed the heavy dark curtains; now the only light in the room is a faint glow from a swirling light just above their heads over the center of the table.

"Please hold the hand of the person next to you, and we will start." They each reached out and held the other's hand around this small round table.

With Kendari's left hand, she held Tori's hand, and with her right hand, she held Heather's. Bill held both Heather's and Tori's; straight across from him sits Kendari.

Kendari started. "Please, will the spirit of Tina make herself known to us sitting at this table? We are here to help you ascend to the next realm and let your spirit rest.

"Your husband and little girl are here," she said as though this were commonplace for her.

The light became brighter and brighter and more clearly formed. Bill and Tori could feel the tears starting to swell up in their eyes. They both knew as did Heather that this might very well be the last time they would all see the spirit of Tina, as it was time for her to move on towards the light.

"Please speak with us, Tina, and let us know what it is that you want," said Kendari.

My darling husband and precious little girl, I want you to know that since that day of my accident many years ago, I have been with you. I have slept by your side and walked with you and gone to school with you, Victoria.

I have felt your pain at my passing and was there when you came to my funeral. I saw the memorial you placed along side the road where I died that day, my wonderful husband.

I have watched you both suffer and cry because I am not there with you as I once was but I assure you that I have been with you every moment since that horrible day.

Heather, I am sorry for causing your accident that night. I asked that deer that night to run out in front of your car. It was the only way that I could get your attention and have you assist me in this attempt to help with my husband and little girl.

Yes, I am the one that caused your accident and ask for your forgiveness. I must move on to the next plain of my existence and move through the light.

There are many more than will need your help once I have traveled to my final place. I have tried to help you and Bill and Tori in your assistance of all the others that will need you to do for them what you have done for me. The puppy, Terra, will provide help to you in a short while with finding these spirits, and then you can meet with Kendari and she will help you to help them move on as I will move on.

If I had not persuaded the deer to run out in front of your car that night, I would still be waiting for a person who has the capability to understand what

I was trying to do when Heather was in the coma. I was communicating with her in a subconscious state. She understood from the beginning that I was trying to communicate with her, but she didn't know that I was also trying to get her to assist me in reaching you and Tori.

Bill, my darling husband, you have grieved for so many years at my passing, and yet you haven't moved on yourself. Like me, you have held on and not let go. Bill, you must now let me go. I must move on, as you must. I could not be more proud of our little girl and how you've raised her. Just look at you, sweetheart—you are the best of your father and myself. My little princess. I have missed you so very much, darling, but now you will have many adventures ahead of you.

With your new puppy, you, your dad, Heather, and Kendari, all of you will be able to help others like me who aren't able to cross over to the other side. Your combined abilities will enable many good spirits to make the final journey as I will today.

Bill, you and Heather make an excellent couple, the manner in which you both work together will be an amazing gift to both others like myself and their families who can't let go of their departed loved ones. Your bond together is a strong one, much like ours was when I was alive.

Heather, please always be a part of Bill's life and that of Victoria's. They both need you in their lives. Please watch over them for me and be a mother to Victoria, she adores you, Heather, and I know you adore her as well.

Kendari, what can I say for someone such as yourself? I thank you more than I can say. You brought this situation to a conclusion. Your insight into the mystical realm of life has excited many like myself, now that they know that they have a chance to move on as I will. Thank you, Kendari.

The form of Tina is starting to fade in and out now as her time has come to an end. The glow of light is fading as are the words Tina speaks to her loved ones.

I will be here waiting for you, my family. Always know that I love you and will be with you in spirit.

And the form of Tina disappears as quickly as it appeared.

All of those around the table are now in tears, including Kendari, and that's saying a lot for a person who is hard around the edges.

They look at each other, stand up and hug one another. The embrace is now one of affection, because they know they've just witnessed a miracle.

Their lives are now forever bound, as friends, family and… who knows!